Winged Horse of Heaven
fallen

R.S. McDonald

Illustrations by Trisha Romo

DEDICATION

This book is dedicated to Christ's Followers of all ages as they learn to wield their spiritual swords in dark places.

CONTENTS

ACKNOWLEDGMENTS

Thank you to my family and friends who have encouraged me to get this story out of my head and into the hands of the people. Special thanks to: Rita, Marian, Marggie, and Jeff who believed this story should be published, and to my husband David McDonald who is not afraid to dream big and fight the good fight.

1- FIRST FLIGHT

Raneous quivered with excitement as he pawed the rich, green grass in anticipation. The young colt adjusted his folded white wings and sighed, "Where are they?" His white coat glistened as he wiggled with impatience. Today had come at long last! He had worked hard everyday strengthening his wings and mastering his flight skills. Chasing colorful butterflies across Brightland's mountain meadows and following his mother through crazy flight patterns in the blue sky all sounded like play but it had a purpose. Now, at last, he was here with the great Heavenly Host preparing to ride out over the Shadowlands. It was the beginning of his training for war and they were waiting for orders.

His mother, Radiance, a beautiful dove gray mare with silver wings, was there as well. A powerful angel with arms and face like rock sat gracefully astride her back. No one would ride Raneous today; he was still too small and he was not supposed to engage in battle yet, but at least he was going. The colt cheered himself with this thought – even if his mother was coming. In reality, Radiance was coming because she was a trusted and skilled war horse who had gained the respect of both angel and demon alike.

This trip's purpose was not to go to battle but more of a scouting party. They were to ride out near the borders of where the Darklands and the Shadowlands met. This order had come from the High King himself, from the heart of the City of Glory. He was going to be mobilizing his faithful children in the Shadowlands soon and send them into the Borderlands. This area held a great stronghold of darkness and the High King wanted to prepare the way for his children before he sent them in. This was to be the first of many trips to the Darkland's border to spy out the Evil One's weaknesses and to begin making the presence of the Light felt in that gloomy, turbulent land.

The Shadowlands, his mother had told him, used to be as bright and unspoiled as the Brightlands where Raneous and all the heavenly beings lived. But through evil deception and bad choices, the people of the Shadowlands had opened the door for evil to enter their realm and so it did. In that moment all was changed! Now the High King fights for his lost children and all of heaven fights with him. For when they opened that evil door, they shut themselves off from their King. All of heaven cried that terrible, tragic day so long ago.

The clear, golden blasts of a trumpet made Raneous jump and look around. His heart beat faster as he trotted quickly to his place. At last the waiting was over! Everyone began to quickly mount their horses and form ranks. Michael, the Archangel, was approaching! Raneous stood as straight as he could beside his mother but couldn't resist peeking around her shoulder to get a better view of the procession. A huge, black, winged stallion led the procession. Silver and gold ribbons glistened in his flowing mane and tail as he approached the waiting party. The bright red banner displaying the golden crown of the King of Kings was held proudly by the angelic standard bearer sitting on the stallion's back. It spread proudly overhead in the breeze. Following close behind came none other than Michael the Archangel. Raneous' gaze was riveted by the sight of the great military leader astride a large and powerful white stallion. The archangel was every inch a warrior. His hard muscled arms seemed to be the size of small trees. A strong, righteous fierceness seemed to emanate from his being.

Raneous tore his eyes away from Michael's face and his heart swelled when he looked at the stallion carrying this massive angel. Palladon, his own father! He was the swiftest and most powerful of all the winged horses. His name had won fame centuries ago – even the Shadowland dwellers had legends about him. To think that his father

3

carried the great military chief! It was enough to swell any colt's head.

However, Raneous did not have much time to revel in his pride long. Michael was giving orders. The archangel had dismounted to address the party. A hush came over the crowd.

"The times grow ever darker in the Shadowlands and the final battle draws ever nearer!" Michael's eyes flashed in triumph and he shouted, "And victory will be ours!"

The Heavenly Host lifted their arms to the heavens, "To the King of Kings!"

Michael shouted heavenward, "To the Prince of Peace!"

"To the Lord of Hosts!" came the deafening response.

"Be all victory and glory and honor and power forever!" All shouted in unison over and over until Raneous' ears rang.

As the din quieted down, Michael continued, "Though victory is sure, there are many battles yet to fight, and the greatest is yet to come. As you know, we are beginning a new campaign and we must begin to penetrate the Borderlands – where the Darklands and Shadowlands meet - in preparation for the King's faithful ones. Now, I stress that we are not going to battle today."

Here Michael paused as his eyes came to rest on Raneous. His eyes softened. "Ahh, Palladon! I see your son is going to follow in your footsteps. It is easy to see that he will be a mighty war horse...WHEN his time has come."

The last phrase he emphasized and Raneous understood that he was not to do anything stupid on this venture. He blushed a bright pink right through his white coat. Luckily, the archangel had already turned back to business and didn't notice.

"We are not going to battle, but we must beware that we will be entering an enemy stronghold. Of course, if we are attacked we will fight but only in defense as we are too few today to actually take ground. Today we will only spy out the land and take stock of the damage done by Darkness.

Michael paused and looked sternly at his band. "I want no heroics today! We are to remain high over the mortal world - above the pull of darkness. And remember, NO demon chasing! They will tempt you to fly low where you will lose your protection – especially you horses. The time is coming but NOT today!"

With that, Michael remounted and looking back, raised a mighty arm, "In the name of the King and for the Kingdom - FORWARD!"

Another trumpet sounded and the mounted troop moved forward, galloping in ranks across the meadow and slowly ascending into flight with a loud thunder of wings. The standard bearer rode beside Michael as he led the way.

Raneous' heart beat wildly as the mountain meadow shrank beneath him as his white wings lifted him into the blue sky. He was leaving all he'd ever known and he was privately glad that his mother was there after all. High above the ground they flew. Higher and higher they went until they were well above any clouds. They headed west with the light of the Brightlands at their backs. Michael, riding Palladon, led them high over the Shadowland world and on towards the churning mass of darkness on the horizon. Raneous took one last glance at his homeland behind him. It was a memory that would stay with him a long time.

2 - THE SHADOWLANDS

They were traveling at incredible speed – faster than any jet airplane. Raneous kept in stride beside his mother but looked with curiosity at the strange world below. They were too far up to actually see the land's characteristics but he could see the shifting shadows moving over the earth's surface. From his vantage point, Raneous could see thousands of miles stretched before him. A burst of light far below and to the left of his vision caught his eye. It was as if a great golden firework had gone off in the middle of a thick fog. The mare noticed it too.

"A great victory has been won for the High King in that place. See how the fog recedes before the light?"

It was true. Raneous could see that where the flash had gone up the fog had rolled back and bright sunshine was pouring through the gap.

"The King's children are beginning to understand the power that the High King has given them over the Evil One and they are learning to use it. When they fight together in unity, that" – the mare nodded towards the bright patch below – "is the result of their labors."

"So that victory was not won by any Heavenly Host?" Raneous felt disappointed.

"Oh yes, we had our part in it too. Don't worry my eager one! You will get your fair share of it. Remember when I told you how the King created mankind in his image long ago before they fell into darkness? Well, by doing that he gave them his creative power through words. With words he created their world and now they have the power to speak light into darkness. This also helps us since it exposes the enemy and weakens him."

Raneous pondered this as he listened to the thundering beat of wings, "But why doesn't the King just do it himself since he has the power?"

"A very good question! If the mortal children of the High King are to regain their lost position with him as rulers and heirs, they must learn how to use the tools he gave them to reign with. It takes wisdom and creativity to rule a kingdom, so the King uses the Shadowlands for their training grounds. When the time comes, the King's children will be ready and equipped to come into their own."

Raneous pondered the shadowy land below him that was in so much turmoil. Flashes of light exploded here and there – signs that the war was constant. The Darkland clouds loomed on the Western horizon; their looming black mass churned and brewed as if to swallow up the Shadowlands if they could. Raneous remembered his mother telling him about how the High King himself had been so heartbroken when mankind had cut themselves off from him by choosing evil; he had made the ultimate sacrifice to get them back. He stripped himself of all his glory and became one of them - a human being. Then at the perfect time in history, he allowed himself to die for their wrongs – somebody had to pay for their wrongs and he was the only one who could. A horrible and painful death it was, but as Creator of the world, he alone was able to defeat Death and the Evil One, the Great Dragon. Then amazingly, he returned to life! This miracle of love opened up a path for his lost children to be able to rejoin their King as rulers and heirs. Raneous sighed. Now it was a fight to reach the King's children, to help them find the path, but the enemy was clever and always capturing them through his evil deceptions. Someday....

The sight of two gleaming, yellow eyes glaring at him from behind a dark cloud jolted Raneous back to the present. Clouds! The dark, angry looking clouds surprised him by their closeness. The colt had been so caught up in his thoughts that he didn't notice when they had lost altitude. They were nearing the Borderlands and the dark, threatening thunderheads loomed all around the scouting party. Raneous glanced back to where those evil eyes had been, but they were gone. Maybe he had imagined them? Raneous shuttered. The wind blew cold here and the air seemed charged with tension. He glanced at the warrior on his mother's back. The angel's jaw was set, his eyes were alert but there was no fear in them. Raneous gulped and tried to look courageous but was dismayed to feel his coltish knees trembling in their strides. He hoped nobody noticed.

Meanwhile, while Raneous struggled with his courage, a black reptilian-like demon glared; its yellow eyes burned with anger as it watched the troop pass. "What did it mean? There were not more than fifty in all so it could not be a full attack. And yet…" The demon clenched its fists, its sharp claws piercing its own flesh in its agitation. "Yet Michael the Archangel led the band. The captain must know of this! But wait!" The demon's dark mind twisted, "What glorious evil can I bestow on this righteous rabble? What knowledge can I wrench from the unsuspecting?" The demon considered the angels. "No, too strong and they never talk. The horses are better game as they have been known to be more vulnerable to the pull of the Shadowlands." The demon grinned cruelly to itself as its eyes fastened upon the white colt.

The demon followed the angelic party careful to stay hidden behind the dark, angry clouds that now surrounded them. A wall of towering blackness loomed directly ahead churning and boiling as if something alive lived within. The wind began to blow and lightning flashed bright against the darkness. The demon nodded its head knowingly. The captain had spotted the Heavenly Host and was brewing a welcome for them. Now would be the perfect opportunity. The demon flexed its claws in anticipation, eyes glowing hot. Licking its scaly lips, it crouched, waiting for the perfect time. With a blood-curdling scream, it lunged.

3 - ATTACKED!

The thunder rolled and the lightning flashed followed by blinding rain. Raneous faltered in his stride as he struggled in the onslaught. The band of angelic warriors was turning to avoid entering the storming thunderhead. Raneous realized he had fallen back and began to make efforts to regain his lost position beside his mother.

"Hurry Raneous!" the words of the mare were blown back to him in the blinding rain. Another lightning crash pounded his ears and pierced his eyes. He struggled to see ahead. Suddenly, a terrifying scream stopped his heart as a horribly painful jerk to his back leg pulled him downward! Down he plummeted desperately trying to regain control, but gravity and a scaly claw were pulling hard on him. Wings flapping crazily, he continued to spiral down, down, down, as the wind whipped around him and evil laughter filled his ears.

"Mother!" he screamed, terrified. The dark clouds boiled up around him as if to consume him.

"Raneous! Raneous!" the mare and her rider broke rank to come to his aid with a fiercely drawn sword. But the white colt could not be seen. The angry clouds had swallowed him up. "Raneous! Raneous!" the two flew back and forth searching and calling. Desperate to find her son, Radiance began to descend into the clouds, but the angel pulled her up gently,

"I'm sorry, but we cannot disobey orders and fly below the clouds." Looking out over the dark cloud cover he sadly added, "We are just going to have to trust the High King on this one."

Radiance bowed her head in sorrow but slowly turned to catch up with the quickly vanishing war band. Softly she whispered, "He is in your hands now High King."

4 - LOST

Raneous opened his eyes. The rain was still beating down in fierce torrents. He lay crumpled in a sticky pool of mud at the foot of a sheer rocky cliff. Terror filled the colt's heart as dark visions of clouds, glowing eyes and worst of all, that evil screaming laughter that curdled the blood filled his mind.

"Mother, where are you?" Raneous struggled to his feet. Silence, except for the sound of sheets of rain beating down on him answered his call. He looked up at the cliff trying to see through the rain. Impossible to climb, he decided, but not impossible for a flying horse! He leapt into the air and with a startled grunt landed heavily on his feet again. Raneous looked with disgust at the black, gooey mud oozing over his small hoofs. "Need to get a better start." He muttered to himself. This time he jumped harder straining for the air.

Splash! Back into the nasty mud and water he landed. "What is wrong with me?" Frightened, he knew the longer he stayed here the less likely he'd be able to catch up with the war band.

"Mother! I'm down here! I'm okay!" Raneous ran back and forth calling up to the top of the cliff the rain lashing his face.

An evil laugh pierced the air. Raneous froze and looked anxiously around.

"It's no use, baby, your mommy has left you!"

Raneous caught the yellow glow of the demon's eyes as he leered at him from an overhanging rock. He shied away quickly.

"You're all alone and wingless, horsey!" continued the voice with another scream of laughter.

"Liar! You lying demon!" Raneous tried very hard to remember he was part of the Heavenly War Host but his quavering voice betrayed his fear.

"Ha!" the demon sneered. "You don't believe me? Look at your back, horsey. You're just a little plow horse now. No more grand rides in

15

the sky for you!"

Raneous looked over his shoulders for his white feathery wings. The shock of the truth hit him. They were gone! Quickly, he craned his neck around the other way trying to see better – nothing. It was like they had never been. Despair reached out to engulf him.

The demon screamed triumphantly, "You're mine, now! You have been doomed to the Darklands! Abandoned by your own kind!" The demon leaped down from his rocky perch with outstretched claws. "I'll bridle you for my own use! And I want some answers too!" it snapped lunging at Raneous.

Raneous dodged the grappling claw. Anger began to rise up in him dispelling the fear and despair that threatened to clutch his heart.

"No! I will never be one of yours! Never!" Raneous lunged towards the surprised demon and rearing up smacked it on its scaly head with his sharp little hoof. The demon yowled in pain and rage holding its head, but Raneous turned quickly and kicked again with his back hooves. The demon rolled away screaming.

And Raneous, almost as surprised as the demon, bolted towards the black woods that seemed to suddenly rise up ahead of him out of the rain.

5 - FOUND

The fog hung like wisps of tangled gray hair among the trees. Raneous stumbled through the misty, old forest. He had been walking forever it seemed and still the black forest kept on. The trees grew so close together that their branches and leaves shut the sky out completely.

"Not that it mattered much, its dark out there too!"

A stray root caught Raneous' hoof and with a squeal he tumbled headfirst into some thorny brambles. Thrashing his spindly legs wildly, he tried in vain to loose himself, but the harder he thrashed he only succeeded in getting himself further entangled in the cruel vines. The more he struggled, the tighter the vines became, gouging the colt's tender flesh.

"I'm lost forever! Not even the High King can find me here!" Big tears spilled down his white face that was now splotched with blood. It was no use struggling against the thorny bush; it held him fast.

"I wonder if I'll die here." He wondered dully if he could die. Heavenly beings were eternal creatures but eternal life may have disappeared with his wings. The darkness closed around him and Raneous gave his exhausted body over to sleep.

*

"Rake the leaves! Milk the cows! Gather the firewood! What am I, slave labor?" the boy of eleven years muttered angrily to himself. He slashed angrily at the tangling vines with his long knife as he picked his way through the woods. "All the wood's wet anyway. I don't know why I bother."

Brian scowled at the two, small, wet sticks he had gathered thus far. But the thought of his uncle's anger pushed him on. He brushed his wavy brown hair out of his dark eyes. Things had never been the same since his mother had married his Uncle Meldron shortly after his father's unexpected death. She had put him off, but the burden of trying to manage the farm by herself caused her to finally give in to his proposals. "Not that it's done her any good!" The thought of his mother's haggard face caused Brian to begin hacking fiercely at the thick underbrush. "He's a no good lazy bum!" he said louder than he meant to.

A flash of white caught his eye. Something was moving in that huge thorn bush! Brian held his breath. These were strange woods. Odd things happened here and legends abounded. The bush moved again revealing a patch of white through its thorny vines. Brian stepped closer, his long knife raised. "Who goes there?" he tried to sound mean and gruff. The movement stopped but he could hear the creature's rapid breathing. It was afraid, he realized.

Stepping closer, he parted the thorny branches with his knife. Brian's brown eyes grew wide in amazement. He gasped, "A horse! No, a colt peered anxiously at him out of the middle of his cruel prison. "Where did you come from?" Brian looked quickly around the thick overgrown forest half expecting to see the colt's owner. Raneous whickered softly to him and began to struggle again. "Why you're stuck, aren't you?" Brian then saw the bloody stains on the white coat where the needle sharp thorns had pierced his flesh. "Well, we must get you out of this mess." Talking softly so as not to alarm the animal, Brian began cutting away the vines that had wrapped themselves around the colt's body. Finally, the last vine fell away and Raneous stepped out of the thorny prison. Shaking his mane, he snorted.

Brian stepped back and expected the horse to run. To his surprise, he didn't. Instead, this beautiful, though very dirty, colt took a few steps towards him and slowly stretched out his head to sniff Brian's brown tasseled hair. Brian stood quietly as he nuzzled his way to his ear.

The soft velvety nose and snuffley breath tickled and he laughed.

This caused Raneous to jump back but not to run. The exploring nose continued to the sleeve of his worn shirt which he experimentally nibbled. The warm breath brushed Brian's hand. The inspection ended at the knee patch of his trousers. The young horse seemingly satisfied, raised his head, looked Brian square in the face, and whinnied. Brian was struck by the intelligent hazel eyes.

What a beautiful horse! Could it be there was no one to claim him? Could he just bring him home like a stray dog? Suddenly the desire to keep this mysterious colt was overwhelming. He could keep him in the old mule shed. What could he tell his uncle? His mind raced. He couldn't tell his uncle. He'd make him into a plow horse for sure. Well, he couldn't leave him here by himself. He'd get lost again or get hurt by some wild animal. But would he come with him? He had no rope or bridle so the colt would have to follow him if he chose.

Brian grabbed up a few more sticks for firewood. It was getting dark and not even his uncle's displeasure could make him stay in this gloomy woods after dark. Turning, Brian beckoned to the young horse. "Come on! We'll get you some dinner." The colt, as if trying to make up his mind, glanced around at the ever darkening woods and then suddenly followed the boy. "He really trusts me." Brian smiled to himself. He hadn't been trusted by anyone in awhile. As boy and horse proceeded homeward, high up in a dark tree two yellow eyes glowed intently.

6 - UNCLE MELDRON

Brian gritted his teeth as his uncle bellowed into his face. Once again, Brian had fallen short of his uncle's hard demands. He had fallen behind schedule and the cows had not yet been milked. He had spent too much time with Thorn – he had decided to name the colt after the bush he found him in. The good news was that after several months his uncle still had not discovered the colt hidden in the old mule shed at the back of the field. "Because he never works in the field." Brian bitterly thought to himself. "All he does is lay around with his jug of moonshine and give orders." But Brian bit his lip and said nothing. He didn't want to draw any attention to the field now.

The colt had become his companion and he found himself

confiding in the horse. Thorn, of course, did not respond, but Brian just felt somehow those large, intelligent eyes understood. He knew that was silly but it comforted him somehow to have someone to tell his troubles to.

Brian had begun waking before dawn to take Thorn to the meadow where he could run as he should. In the early morning darkness with the moon lighting their path, horse and boy made their way through the dark forest to the secluded meadow. Then as the darkness gradually receded, they would play tag in the morning mists. Whinnying, Thorn trotted after the boy to grab his shirt tail in his teeth. Brian would turn then in effort to tag the white colt before he could dart away. Rushing forward or dodging out of reach, Brian laughed and played with Thorn. Of course, the young horse made sure to let the boy tag him sometimes so he wouldn't get discouraged.

After their game, Thorn would crop the meadow grass as the boy stood beside him with his arms wrapped around his graceful neck. This is how they watched the new dawn and it was the best part of the day, and the only peace in the boy's bleak life. It became their ritual. As the sun's rays peaked over the dark, distant hills, Brian reluctantly would lead them back to the stall in the old mule shed. He regretted having to pen Thorn up all day but he tried to reconcile himself with the promise that he would visit the colt throughout the day so he wouldn't get too lonely. Thorn always went willingly back to the stall like he understood the situation.

Now, as he stood before his uncle, Brian knew he was going to pay for his lost time. Today, he had slipped into the shed to visit Thorn and he had gotten so involved in pulling the burrs from Thorn's mane and tail that he lost track of time. He had been telling Thorn about his father. As always, Thorn was a good listener and had nuzzled him gently as he poured out his grief. Now, he would be whipped for his carelessness.

"Are you listening to me, boy?" his uncle roared, blood shot eyes leering into his. Without waiting for an answer, he grabbed Brian by the collar and hauled him outside. To Brian's dismay, he began heading straight for the mule shed.

"No!" Brian desperately protested as he strained against his uncle's grip.

"You can't defy me!" Meldron stopped just long enough to slug the boy in the face.

Brian's head jerked back from the blow and blood spurted from his nose, its coppery taste filling his mouth. He staggered as his uncle jerked him forward once more. Brian's face throbbed in pain and he felt his left eye beginning to swell. Despair filled him as they reached the shed. *"He'll find Thorn and sell him or beat him!"* A moan escaped his lips.

His uncle, however, did not enter the mule shed but dragging Brian with him, headed for the tool shed directly behind it and threw open the door with his free hand. He staggered with the effort, but holding Brian firmly, he retrieved from its nail the long snake-like ox whip.

Brian began to tremble. He had never been whipped with an ox whip. "Please Uncle, I won't do it again!"

Meldron turned and snarled at him, "I'll make sure of that!" His breath reeked of sour moonshine causing Brian to gag. "Take off your shirt now!" Cruel anticipation gleamed in the drunk's eyes. Afraid to disobey, Brian complied as tears coursed down his face and stung his swollen eye.

With the first crack, Brian screamed! The searing pain coursed through his thin frame. The cruel whip cut into his back but also wrapped around to lash his chest. Again came the whip and again. Vision began to blur and he wondered if he would die.

"CRASH!" splintered wood flew from the rotting mule shed wall and then a horse's scream pierced the air.

"Thorn!" Brian turned blurry eyes to see the white colt come crashing through the stall, snorting and rearing in fury. "He's grown!" Brian realized, and though not full grown he made a fearful image.

Meldron stood rooted in shock, mouth open, red eyes bulging as Thorn charged him. Thorn reared up and knocked the drunkard onto his back with a blow to the chest. When Meldron moved to rise, Thorn shook his regal head angrily, snorting and pawing the ground. Meldron found himself pinned. Anger replaced shock and his face turned purple and twisted. Waving the butt of the whip he croaked, "Get him off me!!"

"Thorn, please, let him get up. I'm okay." Thorn stood sternly over Meldron but allowed him to rise. Meldron staggered up, brushed the dirt from himself and suspiciously eyed the horse. As he took in the snow white coat and majestic build, he scowled. Brian watched his uncle warily. His lashes from the whip burned and his head throbbed.

"Been hiding this horse from me, haven't you? Feedin' him MY hay! MY oats!"

"He…I…He mostly eats meadow grass." Brian faltered.

"Mostly don't work! You'll pay me back – both of you - with hard labor behind the plow!"

Thorn continued to stand between Meldron and Brian guarding the boy from further abuse.

"I'm the owner here! I'm in charge here!" Meldron cracked the whip by Thorn's feet causing him to rear with a sharp neigh. "I'll teach you who's boss here!" and he cracked the whip again.

"Don't hurt him!"

Meldron laughed, pleased with himself, and with a final glare at Brian stumped back to the house, whip in hand.

7 -THORN SPEAKS

The merciless sun beat down on Brian's bare head as he strained his thin body to control the plow. Thorn's muscles knotted in effort under his muddy white coat. Flies bit at them and buzzed maddeningly around eyes and salty lips. The field was rocky and the hot sun had dried the earth to the consistency of cement. The plow bit into the crusted dirt causing dust to rise. With a dirt caked face streaked with mud and sweat, Brian looked up into the molten sun.

"I wish it would rain. It never rains when we need it, and when it does rain, it gully-washes taking all the good top soil with it."

Thorn snorted and tossed his head which Brian took as a hearty agreement. "Even Nature works against us, Thorn. It's early planting season and already the sun is too hot and dry for a crop to grow well. It seems to get worse every year. The winter gets colder, the storms more violent, and the summers hotter. At this rate, soon we won't be able to live here at all!" The plow sheared to one side as the blade struck a large stone. "Darn! This row's going to be the crookedest yet!" Thorn whinnied, stopping dead still, his nostrils flaring.

They were at the edge of the field where the old forest loomed up with gnarled roots and branches. Thorn continued to stare intently into the gloom. Brian shivered through his sweat. "What is it, Thorn?" He moved to stand next to the young stallion. Brian stared into the blackness until his eyes watered with the effort. Brian's eyes caught a shadowy movement behind one ancient oak. Thorn saw it too and lunged forward dragging the plow with him.

"Wait!" Brian cried, vainly trying to hold him back. "Thorn stop!" It might be a bear!"

But Thorn was in a fury, rearing up and lunging towards the unknown creature. Brian managed to pull the plow loose from its leather holdings and Thorn broke free with another forward lunge.

A savage scream chilled the hot air. Brian could see the thing retreating before Thorn's onslaught.

"No, Thorn! Wait!" Brian ran after the disappearing horse. "Come back! Don't leave me!" Brian's voice cracked at the thought of losing Thorn. He scrambled after him through the dense, dry underbrush. Brian nearly broke through into the unexpected clearing but the sight before him drew him up short.

Thorn and the ugliest, vilest creature Brian had ever seen were slowly circling each other. The creature looked like something out of a horror story with a black scaly body, gleaming yellow eyes and talon like claws. But the sight of Thorn made Brian's mouth drop.

Thorn seemed to be glowing in the gloom! Light radiated from his whole body. Gone was the mud and sweat of the field and in its place was a white radiance as bright as anything Brian had ever seen! But the thing that made Brian drop to his knees and gasp in wonder were the huge, magnificent wings growing out of Thorn's shoulders.

The two beings were oblivious to Brian's presence as they circled each other intently. The demon, (the word came naturally to Brian's mind) struck first with a shriek of anger. Lunging forward, it tried to reach Thorn's underbelly with its huge claws, but Thorn leaped high with a flap of his wings and landed behind the surprised creature. Before it had a chance to turn, Thorn sent the demon crashing into the base of a huge tree with a fierce back kick. Its scream ended abruptly as its head connected with the unyielding bark. It fell limp to the ground where Thorn gave it one final kick that sent it rolling into the forest brush and out of sight. Satisfied, Thorn turned to the dumbfounded boy.

"Don't be afraid, Brian. He's gone and won't try to hurt you anymore."

Brian blinked. The horse's mouth had moved and he swore he just heard him speak!

"Who...What...What are you? How can you talk?"

Thorn nuzzled the boy's ear. "This is the way I've always talked but you've never understood me until now."

Brian realized the rich voice was definitely coming from the velvety lips that nuzzled him. "Oh, great! Now, I know I've lost it! Too much sun for sure!"

Thorn gazed at him with smiling hazel eyes. "And by the way, my real name is Raneous. Thorn is a good name, but my real name is Raneous."

"Raneous." Brian tried the name on his tongue. "That sounds royal somehow. Are you a royal horse?"

"Well," puzzled Raneous, "I guess not in the way you mean, but I serve the High King."

"He must not be from around here because I've never seen any other flying horses...Oh! They're gone! Your wings are gone! And...and you're all dirty again!" It was true. Thorn from the field was back. Sweat and mud stained the white coat once again.

Raneous looked down at himself and at his wingless shoulders. Brian heard him sigh sadly. "Why did you change?"

"I didn't do anything. It just happened. I don't know why. I'm new to all this too. All I know is when I saw that demon spying on us, I just had to do something. And when I faced him in this glen, I felt a power flow through me and I knew I was supposed to defeat him."

"Well, you certainly did that." Brain remembered the horse's well placed kicks.

Raneous, pleased with himself nodded. "I did, didn't I? My mother would be proud."

"You have a mother?! Well, of course you do. You're not even full grown." Brian quickly added, "But if you have a mother and you serve a King, how in blazes did you get to this God-forsaken place?"

"Its not completely God-forsaken, otherwise I wouldn't be here. And although I don't understand it all yet, I think there's purpose to my being here and today just confirmed it."

"What do you mean?"

"Well, the King I serve is THE KING as in the High King – the Caption of the Angelic Host."

"You mean God?"

"That's exactly who I mean."

"Then..." Brian grasped at the thought, "if you live with God, you're from heaven." This seemed too incredible, but then so did the sight of a flying horse and a so-called demon fighting it out in a deserted wood.

"Not exactly from heaven although I guess you would consider it heaven. I live in the Brightlands which is just outside of heaven as you think of it. Heaven is where the City of Glory is and the High King lives. A small band of the Heavenly Host was sent out to scout out these borderlands where the enemy has become stronger and stronger. We were to assess the damage and report back to the King the condition of the land and the strength of the enemy. The King is going to be sending some of his people into these lands to begin battling back the darkness. Well, we got in a huge rainstorm and I was attacked by one of those creatures you just saw and fell to the ground. The war band lost me and when I awoke I was wingless and alone. Until now, I thought I'd never see them again, but now I think it might just be a matter of time."

They turned to make their way back to the field. Brian picked his way through the brush, "But why would they just leave you like that – you were just a colt!"

"You can believe I've had plenty of time to think about it and the only answer I know is they were obeying the High King's orders. When we left the Brightlands, Michael the Archangel had ordered, by the King's command, no demon chasing and said something about not getting too close to the earth's pull where we would lose our protection

– especially the horses."

"You mean Michael – as in the angel in the ancient stories- led this party of flying horses?"

"Yes, but not just horses, Brian. Each horse (except me) carried an angel equipped with sword and shield. But apparently we horses are susceptible to the pull of darkness. I was along for the training and by far the weakest in the group."

They reached the plow where it had been abandoned earlier. Brian contemplated it sourly. Then his face brightened. "Thorn - I mean Raneous - I'm glad I found you." He faltered, "I mean I'm not glad you got lost but I don't know what I'd do without you now. And something good is happening because even though you lost your wings, I can still hear you talking to me."

Raneous tugged at his shirt tail playfully. "You're a good friend, Brian. We need each other I think."

8 - CAPTURED

The demon cringed as the hot, vaporous breath seared his skin. "You failed me again, Vengol! You, you, vile scum!" the captain shrieked. "I sent you to spy on that farm and what happens? You get beat up by a mere foal!"

"Oh, great Captain Voltar, it was not a normal foal, but a young stallion of the Heavenly Host!" whined the miserable monster. His head was filled with fire from his tree injury.

"You amaze me with your insight," sneered the red eyed captain. "And, I believe, the very same colt you dragged from the sky only to allow to escape! He is a spy, you idiot, placed here by that nosey

Archangel! They baited you like a cursed fish and you swallowed it whole. He must be removed! He is tainting the boy and may destroy all my wonderful hard work in the farmer and even in the area. I will not have my work destroyed! Take reinforcements! Capture the pony – he is but one – how hard can it be? We are strong here and we will remain so!" Pouncing on the cowering demon, Captain Voltar threw the creature from his presence. "Be gone! Don't fail me again!"

*

Raneous munched thoughtfully on the hay Brian had left him. A bit on the dry side, he thought, wistfully remembering the fresh tender grass of the Brightlands. The growing season was drawing to an end. The garden had finally withered and died midsummer. The intense heat scorched the growing plants even when Brian's mother hauled water into it daily. Then as if adding insult to injury, when the much needed rain did come, it was fierce and hard and beat down the garden plants and the wheat growing in the field. Not all was lost but it had been a very poor year. Everything came hard here in the Borderlands. Raneous glanced out the stall's window to stare at the black, churning clouds on the horizon. The people here did not seem to be aware of it. Even Brian had never mentioned it.

Raneous' thoughts flicked back to his encounter with the demon in the woods. He had not seen him since – at least not physically. But he sensed him and others lurking as he and Brian worked the fields on the edge of the dark forest. The eyes of many were watching him, measuring him. He knew they were scheming. They obviously did not want a horse of the High King so deep in their territory. *"What were..."*

"I HATE HIM!" Brian kicked open the stable door. "He can't do this to us!" Tears were mixed with blood on Brian's bruised face. His nose was bleeding. Anger and hatred seeped from every pore in his body as he stood in front of the white horse with hands and teeth clenched. "He's going to kill her one day if I don't take care of him!" Anger turned to a plea, "Help me Raneous!"

Meldron's beatings had become more frequent and more severe as alcohol and hatred consumed his soul, but Brian had changed too. In spite of Raneous' efforts to comfort him, what had first been hurt and fear had now turned to hate and bitterness towards his uncle.

A roar came from the house and a woman screamed, "No Meldron! Don't hurt him!" Brian's eyes grew wide in his bruised face as fear overtook hate.

"Quick! On my back! We must go!"

Meldron's drunken roar grew louder. Brian grabbed the long mane and pulled himself up yelling, "Out the back!" Out of the shed they flew kicking up dust as they headed towards the forest ahead.

"Yooooou! Thash MY horsh...! I'm not done wish yoooou!!" but the cries grew quickly faint as they entered the gloom of the forest.

*

Deeper and further in they went. Raneous slowed to a walk

picking his way through the thick undergrowth while Brian dodged branches overhead. Raneous could feel Brian's body trembling as he rode. *"Fear or anger?"* he wondered.

"I'll kill him, Raneous, before he kills me or my mother."

"Anger."

"Brian, you can't"

"I have every right to."

Raneous sighed, he felt too young to be dealing with this type of stuff. Sure, he wanted to be a great war horse, but this was a war of a completely different kind. *"High King, guide me in this."* "Brian, I am not saying it would not be just in many ways. Evil has taken over your uncle's heart. The Destroyer is at work in him." Here Raneous stopped and looked over his shoulder at Brian, "But Brian, I believe that same Destroyer is at work in you too. You have changed. You're growing hard inside. I'm afraid that if you murdered your uncle that it would also kill you. And of course, murdering someone is never the answer."

"Is there no justice then?" Brian gritted his teeth. "I have listened to you talk about this High King and his good and righteous ways. You're always talking about him sending in his war host, but I have seen little evidence of him around here."

"The High King will bring all things to right in his time."

"I will be dead by then and so will my mother!" spat Brian crossing his arms and looking into the dark forest gloom, but then almost was unseated by a branch in his distraction.

Not a bird sang, but Raneous thought he heard a soft, cruel laugh. He pricked his ears and looked quickly around. Nothing stirred.

"I'm not saying," Brian continued, unaware of Raneous' tension, "that I don't believe you, but I don't believe he really cares about my situation – or yours."

A doubt flickered in Raneous' mind.

"You have been here with me for nearly a full year and no one has come for you. You have been left on your own to fend for yourself. I am just lucky I found you before someone else did."

Raneous snorted, "No! It's not like that!"

"Then tell me how it is my friend."

"I'm not sure....but..."

"Ha!" an evil, triumphant laugh broke his thought. FEAR now enveloped the two travelers like a suffocating blanket. Scaly, reptilian looking creatures dropped out of the dark tree branches. Two, three – no – six demons surrounded Raneous and his rider.

"So!" croaked the biggest of the six. "We meet again. Only now it is you, not Vengol that will pay."

"You have no claim over me, demon." Raneous shook his mane at the intruder.

"No? Well, maybe not yet." The demon smiled slyly and flicked his gaze to Brian. His smile became a sneer. "Take the boy! He is ours!"

Brian went white with fear and shock.

"No! You can't have him!" Rearing, Raneous caught the demon under the chin with a strong hoof while Brian held tight to his mane.

"You!!" howled the creature, "You cannot deprive me of what is rightly mine!" The other demons crept closer tightening the circle and grinning at Brian. "The hate in his heart. It lives and breathes. He has chosen and he is ours!" The demons howled and shrieked as they leapt onto the confused horse dragging the boy from Raneous' back.

Fire blazed from Raneous' eyes in righteous anger, "In the name of the High King, get off!" As he spoke the words, strength flowed into his quivering limbs, FEAR fell away, light radiated from his being and the sound of his beating wings filled the air.

The demons, confused and pierced by the light, reeled back against the trees. But the head demon shrieked, "It is our right! The boy is ours! You have no power over him!"

Sure enough, though Raneous could throw demons from himself, he could not keep them off of Brian. Five demons clawed at the boy, dragging him further away from Raneous.

"NOOOO!" The boy fought and kicked but it was no use. "Raneous help me! Don't let them take me! Please!"

Vengol leered into Raneous' face, "See? You are powerless. We take what belongs to us. You have lost him – unless..." here the demon smiled slyly again. "Unless you would wish to come with him."

"Don't leave me Raneous!" the boy's cries trailed off as they dragged him deeper into the forest.

Go into the Darklands? Everything recoiled in him at the thought. But leaving Brian to the Evil One was equally unthinkable. He wavered for a moment but the decision was clear. "Alright." Raneous lowered his head. "I will go with him."

The demon laughed triumphantly as he immediately produced a bit and bridle. He slipped it quickly over the lowered head. Vengol whispered savagely, "Do not think you will be a hero, foolish one? Those who go in don't come out." He pulled a sack cloth over Raneous' head so that he would be led blind.

It hit Raneous like a thunderbolt that this was what they had planned. This was their scheme. He had fallen into their trap so easily. Despair rose up. He was now in their power. "No," he reminded himself, "They do not own me. My heart belongs to the King!"

9 - THE DARKLANDS

"Captain Voltar, I have succeeded in bringing you the foolish and rash colt! And I have brought you an extra prize –the boy!" Vengol wheezed happily as he pushed Brian bound with chains to the floor. "He is ours."

Brian and Raneous had been brought before the Captain in a cold, dank cave lit with dull red lanterns. Raneous glared at him.

The Captain regarded them both from his stone chair. He grinned wickedly, "Yes, I see my servant Meldron has been working wonders. Soon he will join us as his usefulness comes to an end. The woman, however, is a harder nut to crack, but she will crack. Well, my little maggot, you have finally learned some craftiness. This bothersome pony will no longer be doing any damage! But now we will get some information out of you!" Captain Voltar grinned maliciously at the horse standing before him. He clapped his claws together, "My whip! Bring me my whip!"

A small demon scurried forward dragging a huge whip. Voltar grabbed the whip from the shirking demon and kicked him out of the way. "I know how to make horses talk. Bring me the boy!"

Brian, who had remained crumpled on the floor began to tremble violently as he was dragged before the Captain. Voltar flicked the whip in the air over Brian's head revealing its true nature. Sharp bones and barbs were attached to its leather strands.

"A trick I picked up over the years. Very useful."

Raneous snorted angrily at the demon. Voltar fiercely turned to the horse and hissed, "Now you had better talk or this boy becomes hamburger meat today."

Raneous trembled. What should he do? Brian would die, surely, and yet how could he betray the King's plans?

Brian screamed as the whip slashed through his skin leaving a bloody trail of flesh. Raneous reared up, "STOP!! Stop the flogging!... I will tell you."

Voltar laughed triumphantly, "You see? It's so simple. These horses are so foolish. Out with it or he gets another round!"

With head bowed in shame, Raneous told the great demon of the High King's plan to send his faithful followers to the Borderlands and Archangel Michael's plan to prepare the way for them.

The demon captain's eyes glinted, "Ha! Is that it? I would have thought the King more imaginative in his scheming. No matter, we will be waiting for these newcomers. They will be easily dealt with. Now I think these two need a little hard work to clear their heads. Take them away!"

*

Deeper and deeper they were dragged or pulled down a narrow shaft until Raneous thought they were going to the center of the earth. Suddenly, the close tunnel opened up and he could hear shouts and cursing and the crack of a whip. It was a huge mine. Slaves were carrying rubble and dirt out of various tunnels that branched out from the central room like spokes on a wheel.

"Welcome to your new home!" sneered Vengol. "You will be assigned to the new division that just opened up in the east wing." Brian looked around in dismay. "And you, my boy, will learn to work hard and fast unless you like the feel of the whip on your back! We make your uncle seem like a school boy!"

"I will go with the boy." Raneous sternly told the demon.

The demon hesitated, then roared with laughter, "Of course, of course! The great war horse has become a loyal lap dog blindly following his master. Go, it's your choice."

*

Sweat and foam dripped from Raneous' mud caked body as he strained to pull the cart of rocks up the steep incline. Brian pushed from behind.

"What do you suppose the purpose of all this digging is?" puffed

Brian.

Raneous had been wondering the same thing but did not answer at once. Moving up the other side of the incline, a splash of red caught his eye. It was a horse! In the days they had been in this horrid place, he had seen no other animal, much less a horse.

"I have wondered myself, Brian."

The red horse was growing nearer. The demon behind it cracked a whip, "Get up you lazy brute! Faster I say!"

The red horse, to Raneous' surprise, snarled back curling its lips. "And I will kick a hole in that empty scull of yours if you use that on me again!"

The demon laughed but did not use the whip again. The red horse turned again to the road and saw Raneous. A spark of recognition leapt between the two as each recognized his own kind. Suspicion quickly clouded the red horse's eyes.

"I see the King continues to discard his own."

Raneous stiffened, "I am here by choice."

The red horse continued on past but laughed bitterly, "Well said, white one! We are all here by choice."

10 - PRISONERS

It seemed neither night nor day in the deep caverns of the Darklands. The red glow from the torches and lanterns was the only light cast over the underground cavern. All sense of time was lost as the days blurred together. Shovel rocks into the cart; pull the cart from one end to the other and empty it. Then return to do the whole mindless, backbreaking routine over again.

Once Brian even asked a guard what the purpose of this whole project was. He was rewarded only with shrieks of laughter and some angry blows to the head with the butt of a whip. "You're not working hard enough if you have anything left to think with!" the demon bellowed as he slammed Brian against the rough wall of the cavern. Brian didn't dare ask again.

Raneous did notice that most work seemed to be concentrated in the east tunnels. It was like they were moles tunneling through the underground.

"If I wasn't so hungry and thirsty, I would say that we were dead." Brian heaved a particularly large rock into the cart. "Even the demons seem to know that if we aren't fed and watered they won't get any work out of us."

Raneous didn't answer but waited patiently as Brian filled the cart. There wasn't anything left to consider. Every day was the same. Brian, along with countless other sorrowful souls were taken and placed in large, individual cages and locked in for the night – if it was night. When the next day was to begin, the prisoners were given a watery, tasteless porridge with a cup of water. This same fare was given again at the day's end. Water, however, was given at midday as well. Unlike Brian, Raneous was not caged but left to himself. He always chose to spend the night in front of Brian's cage. Hay and water were begrudgingly brought to him. The weary horse pondered this and felt that somehow there was a secret here. "What had the red horse said? 'We were all here by choice...'"

WHAM! The whip butt hit Raneous right between the eyes. "I'm talking to you! Are you now deaf too?"

Raneous reared back in startled anger. The demon stepped back hastily but grinned knowingly, "You hate me don't you? Where is your High King now? He doesn't care about you or this filthy wretch you have tied yourself to. No one can save either of you. You've been abandoned for good now, you know. You betrayed your King so you have been thrown away like garbage!"

Raneous glowered at the demon and realized it was Vengol, the same creature who yanked him out of the sky so long ago. "If it wasn't for you, you son of dirt, I wouldn't be here!" Anger filled the horse's heart so that he trembled. Just then he heard a laugh. The red horse was laughing at Raneous. The demon too sneered at him, "No one ever leaves!"

That night after Brian had fallen into another exhausted sleep, Raneous went searching for the red horse. His search was quickly over. He found the horse about twenty yards away in his own iron cage equipped with trough and manger.

"So, you've come at last. I've been expecting you." The torch light gleamed on the fiery red coat making it look blood red. There was no kindness in the voice.

"I want to know your story. Why are you here? Who are you?"

The caged horse appraised the other with a cold eye. "I am Rune." he said at last like it didn't really matter. "I was once like you; idealistic, full of the noble deeds that I could do for the High King." the last two words he spat.

Ignoring the insult, Raneous pressed in, "What happened to you?"

Rune did not answer at once but considered Raneous as though sizing him up. "Very well. I will tell you my story. It will help you see what type of person the High King really is!"

11- RUNE'S STORY

"I was a great war horse very, very long ago. Every angel desired to be my rider. Michael the Archangel and I slew legions upon legions on the dark side. None could match us. One day I was summoned by the High King himself.

'You are the greatest war horse in the Brightlands.' He told me. 'Therefore, I have chosen you for a very dangerous and unique mission.'

The power to make war was given to me and my mysterious

rider. This rider I had never seen before. He was dressed in armor as a silver knight. The visor of his helmet was tightly shut and he never opened it. In his hand he carried a great flaming sword. The honor of being chosen for this mission was great and we rode out with great fanfare and trumpets blaring. We also rode out alone." Rune paused as he remembered that bright moment so long ago.

"That was the last I saw of the Brightlands. My rider never spoke but guided me silently. We descended into the clouds of the Shadowlands. We flew with great speed from one nation to the next, from one kingdom to the other. Wherever we went, war broke out. Faster and faster we flew over the Shadowlands, and as we flew, peace was no more. The cry of dying innocents began to pierce my ears and my heart. I began to realize we were not destroying demons and monsters with this power as I had assumed. We were causing people and nations to fight each other, destroy each other, and injure each other. The Evil One and his minions shrieked and laughed in triumph and they rushed in to assist in the slaughter. HATE, GREED, LUST, MURDER; they were having a glorious feast in our honor!" Rune's eyes narrowed at the memory. It was several moments before he continued.

"All of the Shadowlands was at war. Smoke from the burning cities filled the sky and the streets ran with blood. Who would survive? Why would the High King ask me to destroy the very people we had been working so hard to save? Evil and cruelty were running rampant. I thought the King loved these people. Didn't he, himself, die for them at one time?" Anger began to flare from Rune's eyes. "He betrayed me!"

"Who did?"

"The High King! He turned me over to the enemy! As I watched the devastation of war take hold of the land below me I began to wonder who my rider was. I became more and more agitated the more I thought about it. He was not like any I'd known. Finally, I stopped and demanded, 'Show yourself, rider!' At first, he did nothing but kept signaling for me to move on. 'No! I must know who you are!' I turned my head to look at him as he sat astride my back. Slowly, he raised his visor and..." Rune shuddered at the memory. "It was no angel leading me in destruction. What met my gaze were the empty sockets of a grinning skull!

'No!!' I screamed and reared up trying to throw the cursed thing from my back! To think we had been treated with so much honor and fanfare as we left the Brightlands! If only they had known the hideous creature that was hidden behind that shimmering armor, it would not have been so.

But the High King knew! He had planned this whole mission. The host had blindly waved us on to our noble deeds in service to the King. I might as well have been working for the Dragon! That day, I chose not to serve the High King anymore. At least here I know who is who.

Well, I refused to ride any further with that death-like monster, so he just dismounted and continued on his way through the land. I wandered aimlessly for a time. I could no longer fly. Shorn of all my previous glory, the anger in my heart grew daily and finally the demons were able to capture me. But I would rather be here than serving one who would use me and then betray my trust."

Raneous shook his head. It didn't make sense. The whole terrible story made no sense. Was the High King cruel and uncaring as Rune seemed to believe?

"And now you are here as well. You have been betrayed just as I was. You have been left behind."

"How do you know how I got here?"

"Oh, it's pretty easy to see. You're young. I can see that and I can see the way you've befriended the boy. It's not hard to guess that you got left behind somewhere and the boy befriended you. Remember, I've wondered far in the Shadowlands. I had plenty of people try to harness me or befriend me. I would have none of them. I trust no one."

Raneous thoughtfully made his way back to the sleeping Brian. Rune was caged because he turned his heart against the King. Brian was caged because he hated his uncle and he didn't serve the High King."*And I will be caged if I allow myself to hate with bitterness!*"

However, Rune's story greatly disturbed Raneous. How could it be true? It went against everything he was taught and yet here he was also seemingly left behind and forgotten by all. Not even his mother had come after him. Loneliness crashed in upon him as doubts began to shout, "*You have been abandoned! You'll never leave this hideous hole because no one cares! You are doomed forever! You will never see the Brightlands again!*"

But one thought presented itself quietly but persistently, *"You're not caged."* Raneous clung to that thought. Hope! The evil powers could not hold him because they had no foothold in his soul. Wouldn't this in some small way also indicate that he was not abandoned completely? Raneous took that thought and pushed forward with it. *"And what if a choice could be reversed? What if a person un-chose their decision to hate or not believe? Do we just get one chance? If someone died for you out of love, would that person just give you one chance?"*

Raneous worked this over in his mind. Still, he couldn't make sense out of Rune's tragic story. It did seem like a horrible betrayal, and yet what if there was a piece of the story missing? As Rune even said, the High King had sacrificed all for his beloved creation. He had given his life. War and innocent blood being shed didn't seem right and yet the High King had sent them. Maybe the real story was that it was Rune who had betrayed the High King's trust. After all, the High King had trusted him with a very unique mission. It was all very confusing and complicated and it made his head hurt. *"Do I believe in the integrity of the High King or do I believe a disillusioned war horse"'* Raneous decided that, in spite of the evidence, that for now, he'd bet on the King.

12 - THE SECRET TO FREEDOM

Brian grew pale and gaunt from the endless labor and malnutrition. His lips cracked and bled from his efforts to moisten them with his tongue. Life on the farm didn't seem so bad compared to this slow torture. Muscles ached constantly and thirst became a living thing that breathed fire in his veins. It seemed that his past life belonged to another person. The only thing keeping him in reality was Raneous, but the great white horse suffered as well. His ribs showed, though Brian noticed that his muscles grew stronger and bulkier. The tasteless gruel hardly touched Brian's hunger. When the demon's declared it night, he dreamed about piles of mash potatoes swimming in creamy white gravy; fresh squash and carrots from the garden, hot roasted chicken sprinkled with rosemary and, of course, water. Water! Lots of water! He dreamed of bubbling fountains and fresh, clear mountain streams laughing and gurgling as they bounded down the hillside.

"I'm going to die, Raneous." He said it with quiet certainty as he lay one night on the floor of his cage.

Raneous was becoming very concerned about Brian. His hollow eyes and sunken cheeks did not speak well of the boy's health. Somehow he needed to get him out of this demon hole. Raneous had continued to mull the puzzle of himself and Brian over in his mind, but only one grain of truth seemed to stand out. Choices. This whole world seemed to be based on choices. Suddenly, with a burst of insight Raneous blurted, "Brian, do you hate your uncle?"

Brian turned his head slowly to regard his friend, but even Raneous saw the spark of fire in the boy's eyes as he remembered the man.

"Yes." It was said with dead conviction. Brian turned his eyes away from Raneous and stared up into the darkness. "I hate him with everything in me!"

Raneous began in earnest, "Brian, I believe this prison is the state of your soul. That hatred has given The Evil One the right to take you captive."

"How do you think that? You're here too."

"Yes, I'm here but I am not in an iron cage, nor do they put their hands on me. I can go wherever I wish." Raneous was growing excited as his thoughts took shape in his mind.

"So you're going to leave me, aren't you?"

"No! No! Brian – never." The horse shook his head emphatically. "Just listen. You have chosen to hate and therefore you are here as a prisoner. But...." The horse looked earnestly at Brian. "If you were to choose to forgive your uncle I believe you could leave this place."

"Never!" the force of Brian's words surprised the horse. "How could I after all that he's done to me and my mother?" Hot tears welled up and made white streaks down his grimy face. "I can't, Raneous. It's not in me to do it."

Raneous stamped his hoof impatiently. Time was growing short for Brian. He had to turn him while the boy still had the strength. The boy didn't understand the urgency of his situation. The conviction of TRUTH struck Raneous and he spoke boldly, "Then because you murdered your uncle in your heart, and let hatred consume you, you will be held captive here until you die, a prisoner of your own hate, and at your own choice." Raneous breathlessly watched the boy as his words and their horrible reality sank in.

The boy stared straight ahead, his breath coming faster. Then his face crumpled and tears began to flow. Not tears of anger, but real tears of hurt, pain and sorrow. The knot in his heart began to loosen. Tears and more tears of a wounded and broken heart flowed out. Brian began to wail. He curled up as one in extreme pain hugging himself and rocking back and forth. And still he wailed. It was the voice of years of hurt and abuse and bitterness that had been locked up in his heart. It was the pain of the realization of what he'd become. That in so hating his uncle, he had become like the very man he despised.

Raneous watched this progression in amazement and yet it seemed to progress in the right direction.

"Help me, Raneous! I'm lost and I can't save myself!" Brian continued to wail and began to pound his fists against the bottom of his cage. "I don't want to hate, but how do I change?" the boy was racked with sobs as he continued to rock back and forth on the ground.

"You must let the High King carry your sorrows and heal the wounds." The words were there before he knew what he was saying. Yes, of course! The High King had defeated Evil by taking it all on himself when he had died!

"TRAITOR!" the scream seemed to rip the air. "You can't do this, you little brat! You've already made your choice and it's too late!" The demon leapt on top of Brian's cage fuming with anger at Raneous. "He's ours! No one leaves here! And YOU..! You hunk of horse meat will soon be mine as well! It's just a matter of time! No one escapes the Darklands!"

"Brian! Don't listen to it! It lies. Someone did escape the Darklands once - the High King!"

The demon sputtered, "Foolish boy, do you think YOU could follow in the path of the High King? You are a murderer; he is a King!"

"It doesn't matter, Brian." Raneous spoke clearly, "Anyone who chooses can follow the High King, but you must decide for yourself."

Brian, who had been holding his head in confusion suddenly looked up at the demon. "I choose to give the High King my pain and hatred if he'll take it."

The demon stared in horror, mouth gaping, as Brian's cage began to sparkle with light. Clean, bright, twinkling light shimmered on all the bars. The demon screamed in pain as the light touched his skin and he leapt from the top of the cage howling in rage and fear. The light grew stronger and the bars began to glow white hot. They began to melt and lose shape. Within seconds the last glowing drop had disappeared into the dirt. There was no trace of the cage anywhere. It was completely gone!

13 - CAPTAIN VOLTAR

Both Brian and Raneous stood dumbfounded; both looking at where the iron cage had once held Brian captive.

"Raneous, look! Your wings! You have wings!"

"Look at yourself Brian!" Brian looked down and he was clothed in a white tunic with black breeches and soft leather riding boots. A silver sword hung at his hip. His countenance was bright, all confusion and pain gone.

"Come Brian!" Raneous pranced in anticipation. "There are others here whom we can possibly help! Up on my back!"

"Wow! Do you ever quit growing? You're huge!" But he struggled up and wound his fingers into the long flowing mane.

A general howling noise rose from inside the cavern and echoed off the walls as the demonic host began to realize the situation. A heavenly being was in their midst and was accompanied by the POWER. Demons ran in circles around them and scurried here and there, but none tried to take hold of the great white horse and his rider.

With a great flying leap, Raneous landed on the top of a great cliff overlooking the cavern floor. "Hear us you prisoners of darkness! All is not lost! You too may have freedom if you but choose to serve the High King. You are prisoners of your own black hearts, but if you choose to give it to the King and become his servant, you can leave this cursed place!"

"HA!" Raneous recognized Rune's cold laugh. "Think twice prisoners. Beware! The High King can't be trusted. You never know what he's up to. With the Great Dragon, however, you always know what he is about. There are no guarantees with the High King!"

Prisoners began shouting and some began to argue back and forth while some began to weep. White light began to shimmer here and there as prisoners declared, "I will serve the High King!" Others could be heard wailing, "Have mercy! Have mercy!"

The light continued to increase and soon the wailing turned to shouts of joy as people were freed from their prisons both inside and out.

Then a foul smelling smoke began to churn and boil out of the East tunnel as Captain Voltar entered the cavern.

"Who has DARED disturb my domain?" The great demon shook his clawed fist at Raneous and Brian still positioned on the cliff. "You have caused too much trouble and now you will pay!"

The newly freed prisoners began to quake in fear. "Draw your sword." Raneous said softly to Brian. The sound of unsheathed metal rang across the cavern. Brian felt strength and power surge down his arm and into his whole body. Everyone grew quiet at the sight of the sword held high overhead.

"Servants of the High King!" Raneous addressed the crowd. "You are no longer helpless slaves but now have the power of the High King within you. Draw your swords and fight your enemy for you will surely have victory!"

Raneous glanced back at the boy, "Now Brian, we will face this Voltar!" With a mighty leap Raneous launched himself off the cliff and descended swiftly to the cavern floor between Voltar and the people. The demon's foul breath made Brian's eyes water but he held his sword ready. Something about the stench tweaked Brian's memory. The odor was somewhat familiar though very intense. Uncle Meldron! His uncle had reeked of alcohol. But this was much more than moonshine breath; this was the putrid smell of all addictions.

Already, the new servants of the High King were finding their strength. Demonic howls and squeals of pain were growing louder. Captain Voltar spewed great clouds of foul black smoke as he raised himself to meet Raneous in battle.

"You will never win! We are many and you are but one! You are DOOMED!"

"NO! It is you that is doomed! I understand now that you hold a stronghold of addiction but that power is broken today! The people have chosen and you have lost. Your day of judgment is at hand! To the High King! NOW Brian!" he shouted.

Raneous leapt toward the monster as the scaly creature lashed out with his talons. Smoke choked Brian but the boy ducked and leaned forward to plunge the sword into the creatures exposed underbelly. The sword flashed white fire as Brian felt the scales give way to the searing metal. The great demon reeled back in fury and pain screaming, "NOOO! You cannot defeat me!"

"Look! He's shrinking!" The demon, still slashing wildly, was now only half his former size.

"Again Brian!" Raneous wheeled around with Brian raising his sword, this time aiming for the creature's heart. The demon turned

63

suddenly and the sword sliced through its scaly forearm instead. The arm fell to the floor and withered away.

"Is there nothing to these creatures?"

"They are only as powerful as people are deceived into making them." Raneous wheeled again. "One last time, Brian!" Brian raised his sword again.

The vile creature continued to shriek in rage, "I am Voltar! You can't kill me!"

Brian leaned low over Raneous' neck. Voltar had shrunk so small Brian wondered if he could reach him. Raising his sword back, he swung it in a low arch slicing through the air. The sword burned bright as it sliced open the foul creature's belly. Black grey slime spewed out of the demon's gut and it began to scream, "NO! NO! I won't go back!" The demon writhed on the floor gnashing its teeth at Brian. Smaller and smaller it continued to shrink until it was no bigger than a large rat wallowing in its own stinking bile.

Raneous reared high, Brian holding tight. "Voltar! Be gone from this place!" A sickening crunch and its head was crushed by Raneous' hoof.

Instantly, fireworks seemed to go off all over the caverns. Demons began cowering and running for the tunnels. "The Light! Not the Light! OW! OW!" Shrieking and gibbering, they ran for the dark tunnels. In complete madness they ran clawing and tearing at each other in their effort to get out of the light.

Raneous looked around. The victorious cheered and clapped each other on the back. Only a few cages remained on the floor, each with its prisoner looking sullenly out of his cage, watching the events with suspicious eyes. Rune was there as well looking coldly at Raneous. Raneous approached his cage.

"I see the High King has chosen to grant you victory today. Just wait! Today you served for good but tomorrow you may serve for evil. Such is the unpredictable nature of your King."

Raneous met the fiery gaze and said coolly, "Rune, did it ever occur to you that you may not understand the complete picture? How can you so easily lose faith in the goodness of our King?"

"Your King! He is mine no longer." Rune seemed to hesitate for an instant but his eyes flashed in anger, "No! I know what I know. If you had been treated the way I've been treated, you would agree. Go! Take your people and let me be. You have not seen the last of me." With that, Rune turned his back and would speak no more.

"The choice is yours." Raneous sighed and turned away. "Come Brian, we need to lead these people out of here.

14 - THE ROAD TO FREEDOM

Brian looked around the cavern thoughtfully, "Look Raneous, there's a road that leads upward at the far end of this cave. It seems that light is coming from that shaft now.

Raneous nodded, for a road that he had never noticed before was now bathed in soft shafts of light from somewhere above. It was certainly the way out. "Follow me all you servants of the High King!"

There was some bustling around as the victors cheerfully

assembled themselves into marching ranks. Raneous' heart swelled as he looked at the beautiful sight. Faces bright and full of hope met his. The King's army, arrayed in white fell in behind the great winged horse and his rider. Someone struck up a chant and others quickly picked it up as they marched upward and out.

Hail! Hail!

To the High King!

Victory comes,

It rides on his wings.

Death and addiction are no more,

He seals our hearts,

We wield our swords.

Upward, upward they climbed. They were a magnificent sight as they emerged at last, voices ringing out against the cavern walls. Sunlight glinted off their swords and white tunics as they marched out of the cave's dark mouth and into the bright daylight. They blinked in surprise and they began to shout and laugh with joy because the black forest had changed! Shading his eyes, Brian looked around. No longer were the woods dark and brooding. Great beams of light had broken through to the forest floor. Here and there soft patches of green grass were already springing up. The dark churning clouds had receded and grown much smaller. Raneous halted in a large clearing and turned to address the people. The sunlight gleamed on his snowy white coat and feathery wings. A hush fell over the ranks as they gathered to listen.

"My fellow servants! Today you have chosen a new life and a new King. Today you were delivered out of the darkness that bound you. And just as importantly, you have learned how to defeat that darkness. Remember always who you are and who you belong to. When you draw your swords darkness trembles because of its POWER. The enemy may try to recapture you. Be on your guard and believe no lies. We have won a great victory in the Borderlands this day. A great stronghold has been broken! Now it is up to you to keep the Light of the High King shining brightly, thus keeping the darkness at bay. Go to your homes and to your towns. Be strong and encourage each other. The High King is ever faithful and he will return for his children."

A young man stepped forward, "How can we ever thank you or the High King? I am eternally grateful."

Raneous looked at the man's earnest face. "Go and teach others how to fight the Evil One, the Great Dragon. Those that you find in captivity, tell them the hope that is theirs if they choose. Next to loving him, helping the King bring back his lost children is the best thing you could ever do for him."

"We will do as you say, won't we?"

"We will!" came the cry in unison.

With that, they began to disperse to their different ways, some talking and laughing together; others walking slowly and examining their new swords seriously.

Brian, from his vantage point astride Raneous watched them go and was struck by their diversity. Young and old, men and women, people of all races, the Evil One was no respecter of age, race or gender. He wanted to destroy them all. Finally, Raneous and Brian were standing alone in the clearing listening to the sound of the birds twittering in the trees. How long had they been prisoners in the Darklands? Brian looked around. It was Spring! Brian passed his hand over his face.

"I feel I've been gone a lifetime." He looked down. "Hey!" My sword and white clothes are gone!"

"Just as my wings are gone again."

Brian studied himself; he was wearing a clean blue shirt with crisp tan trousers.

"You've been given a new start, Brian. Don't worry; your sword is there when you need it. Let's go home and see what we find."

15 - HOME

Brian and Raneous looked out over the low lying pine branches at the small farm spread out before them. It had just rained that morning a soft gentle rain, and the fresh air smelled of damp earth.

"Mmmm!" Brian inhaled deeply. "I haven't smelled fresh air and clean dirt in forever!"

"Are you ready?"

Brian had been wondering how he'd feel when he had to face his uncle. He was grateful to know he no longer felt any hatred towards his uncle, but he must stay on his guard. "Ready as I'll ever be, I suppose."

Raneous stepped out into the damp field and started towards the small farm house. Just then the back door slammed and Brian saw his mother cross the yard towards the chicken house carrying a bucket of chicken feed.

"Mother!" Brian slipped off Raneous' back and began running across the field.

The woman started at his voice and turned to see her boy running across the back field towards her. "Brian? Is it you?" In her haste she dropped the chicken feed but ignored it. Brian could see her tired face light up as she ran out to meet him. "Brian! You're alive! Oh thank God!" She threw her arms around him as they reached each other half way. She began to laugh and then cry and laugh again holding Brian as tight as she could. It was a joyful reunion. "I thought you were dead!" She looked again in disbelief into her son's eyes. The happy woman only then noticed the horse. "I see you still have Thorn. My, how he's grown! He's a full grown stallion now."

"He saved my life, Mother." Brian looked towards the house. "Is Uncle Meldron here?"

"No, son. Two days ago he dropped dead of a heart attack. He was buried yesterday."

Brian looked at his mother. Her eyes were sad but there was a peace.

"Try to forgive him, Brian. He was being controlled by a greater force than himself."

"I know….and I have."

Raneous had been quietly watching this reunion and suddenly a wave of loneliness washed over him. He wanted to go home. He wanted to see his own mother again and the green meadows of the Brightlands and…the High King. A doubt nagged at his mind. Would he receive him? He had betrayed him to the demon Voltar to save Brian.

"The door that leads home is within you. Find the door and open it." The words came softly and lit upon his mind. His heart beat faster. It was time to go.

"Brian!" The boy turned smiling at Raneous.

"It's time for me to go home."

The boy's face clouded, "Now?"

"Who are you talking to Brian?" his mother looked at him puzzled.

"My horse. I…I guess you can't understand him."

"Everything will be okay, Brian, and I know I will see you again, but its time for me to go." Raneous walked over and nuzzled the boy who then threw his arms around his powerful neck and held him tight.

"You can't leave! What will I do without you?" Tears sprang unbidden and ran down his face. Brian buried it in the thick white mane.

"I will miss you!" The tears dripped off his nose and into Raneous' mane.

Raneous nuzzled the boy's ear, "And I will miss you, but I'll be back. It's not over. Remember who you are, Brian, and who you serve. Remember!" Raneous turned slowly towards the woods. He looked back and Brian waved with one arm, his other arm around his mother. The great stallion turned and entered the green forest.

16 - THE RETURN

Raneous had traveled swiftly. Some strange urging inside kept him going. The sound of running water caught his ears and he eagerly moved towards it. A small bubbling brook laughed and gurgled its way around and over some smooth rocks. Raneous gratefully lowered his head to drink.

"The way is inward." Raneous raised his head quickly, mouth dripping.

"Well," he muttered to himself, "I guess if it's inward I can quit moving." The brook gurgled at his feet. He looked around. All was peaceful. Raneous squeezed his eyes shut. Now, just the sound of the water invaded his thoughts but it was soothing and he let his mind float along on its sound.

"Where is this door?" In his mind's eye, he could see the forest around him. Suddenly, his mother stepped out of the trees. Raneous opened his eyes and she disappeared.

"Inward."

Puzzled, he shut his eyes again. His mother was standing there once again. *"You're almost home, my son. You must find the door."*

"I don't understand! What is this door?"

"It's the door into the eternal realm and all eternal beings have access to it because it's connected to their spirit. You are caught in the mortal realm's pull. Remember when you fought the demons how you got your wings?"

"Yes."

"You are connecting with the eternal realm and the King's power when you do so. But it is possible to maintain that connection all the time and when you do, the door is open and you can return to the eternal realm. It's an alignment of all aspects or parts of your spirit with the High King's spirit. When that happens, your soul and body follow."

"Total alignment?"

The mare's velvety voice was patient. *"Think of yourself as a beam of light lining up with another beam of light who is the High King. That alignment is submission, or the willingness to follow the High King's ways over your ways. As every part of your being submits to the love and guidance of the High King, your beam of light merges with his. Whatever he does you do. You have perfect communication with him and always know what he wants. There is no more fear and no more wondering."*

Raneous squeezed his eyes tight, "One with the High King." He muttered. Nothing happened. He tried to concentrate harder.

"No, it's not like that. It's a letting go and receiving the High King."

Raneous relaxed. He could still see in his mind's eye his mother and the forest. "I give my all to the High King forever." The outline of a door began to form in the air. Wooden posts and a crossbeam stood freely on the grass, but the wooden door remained shut. Raneous' heart beat faster. There it was! The appearance of the door began to change. Brilliant beams of light were forcing their way around the edges and through the knotholes. He opened his eyes, but the door disappeared.

"Come back!" Raneous shut his eyes again fearing the door would be lost. To his relief the door remained but the light had gone.

"Align yourself with the King."

Raneous again relaxed and imagined himself merging with the Light and Love of the High King. The door began to glow again. Then something happened. Memories began to present themselves to

Raneous; his heartbreak and loneliness of being lost in the dark forest; his fear of being forever forgotten; his doubt and confusion about Rune's tale. As each memory presented itself he let it go. As he released it, the light around the door swallowed it up. The memories of the Brightlands began to flood his mind. The green meadows, his father, Palladon, – everything.

Suddenly, a blinding beam of light formed in front of the door. Raneous moved towards it until it surrounded him. A loving Presence began to bathe every part of his being. He could feel it flowing into every thought and every cell of his body. Light radiated out of every cell of his body; his white coat and wings shone like lightning. For the first time since he was a foal and maybe ever, Raneous felt absolute peace.

"I am Raneous of the Heavenly Host, servant to the High King!" The words rang from his heart and instantly the door flew open and a brilliant blue light that sparkled like diamonds poured out onto the forest floor. Raneous' eyes opened and the door and the light in all its glory were still there flooding the tender grass in dazzling blue light. Raneous took a deep breath and plunged though.

17 - THE HIGH KING

The blazing blue of the sky, the rich, green grass and the brilliant flowers of the Brightlands dazzled his eyes. But before he could think any further, the High King himself was standing before him.

"Well done Raneous!" the booming rich voice reverberated with joy and pride and it nearly overwhelmed the stallion. "Well done!"

Raneous gazed into the face of his King. Deep, deep love and the wisdom of the universes shone out of the King's eyes. The stallion had to look away. Something tickled his mind. What was it? Then he knew. He blurted out, "High King, I betrayed you!" Raneous shamefully bowed his head and stood there dejectedly.

"How so faithful one?"

"I...I told the demon, Voltar, about your plans to penetrate the Borderlands. I ruined your plans."

"And why did you speak of this to the demon?" The King's voice was gentle.

"He was going to kill the boy, Brian, and it seemed the only way to save him."

"And did I ever swear you to secrecy on the matter?"

Raneous paused and looked up at the King, "No, Sire, you never did."

"Then how did you betray me? You chose to trust me and you acted in love towards my lost child."

"But I spoiled your plans, Sire."

The High King threw back his head and laughed whole-heartedly. Raneous gazed at him in wonder.

"No, my true servant, you did not spoil my plans. Why actually, you fulfilled them!"

"I don't understand."

"That was the reason you were allowed to go on that scouting trip. I knew the demon horde couldn't resist a colt like you and with Michael leading the pack, their suspicions would be aroused. Oh, it was risky, but I believed you had the mettle to make it back."

Raneous could again feel the love and pride of the High King in him and it washed that last tinge of doubt away.

"You knew the plan from the start. First, we wanted to find out the enemy's strengths and weaknesses in the Borderlands. Second," the High King raised his two fingers, "we wanted to let our presence be felt to prepare the way for my faithful ones. Third, we wanted to send my servants into the Borderlands to spread my Light and push back the darkness. All of these objectives were fulfilled in you. You not only discovered the enemy's stronghold of addiction that has gripped that region for years, but you discovered where the weakness was, learned how to fight it, taught others how to fight it, overcame it, and all but destroyed it."

Here the High King grinned at Raneous. "By overcoming that stronghold, you sent hundreds of my servants into the land equipped with swords and a song of freedom on their lips." The High King laughed again, "Voltar thought I would be sending outsiders in. He never dreamed that his own prisoners would be delivered right out from under his nose and be the very people who destroyed his stronghold."

The King paused and looked intently at Raneous, "Here is a simple but powerful truth. My plans are for all to see if they choose, but the details of how they will be accomplished remain a mystery to most. Only to those who truly go after my heart do I reveal myself to."

Raneous thought of Rune still in his iron cage, "Then I was right in saying to Rune that there was a piece of his story missing."

"Ah, Rune, my fiery one," the King sighed. "We may yet save that one. There is always hope."

Raneous' mind raced. It was so clear now. The High King had always been in control. He was so clever and smart (he was the Creator of all things after all) and yet Raneous might have spoiled it all by succumbing to his own hatred and bitterness. Yet the King had risked it because he believed that he, a young colt at the time, could make it back.

The High King beckoned to Raneous, "Come and walk with me." Together they walked quietly for a few moments while Raneous drank in the sights and smells of the Brightlands he had missed with every fiber of his being. They presently came to a small apple orchard and the smell of the luscious fruit made Raneous' mouth water. The fruit of the Brightlands made Shadowland food seem like sawdust in comparison. The King smiled, reached up and picked two beautiful red and gold apples – one for himself and one for Raneous.

Chewing in rapturous bliss, Raneous said around his apple, "I think I've died and gone to heaven!" - a phrase he had picked up from Brian.

The High King burst out laughing and said, "Well, you haven't died, but you did go to heaven!" The King chuckled again to himself and then grew serious. "That actually brings me to what I wanted to discuss with you." He looked kindly at Raneous.

"You and I actually have something in common that is very unique to a Brightlander." Raneous pricked his ears in surprise because what could he have in common with the High King? The King smiled at Raneous' apparent surprise, "Do you remember that I gave up my position as High King to be born as a human in the Shadowlands?" Raneous nodded but still was not following the High King's train of thought. The King placed his strong, sure hand on Raneous' forehead and turned to face him. "You and I both grew up in the Shadowlands. You were not born there as I was but we both understand the ways and thinking of the Shadowlanders as only a native can and that comes by living and growing up there. No one else who was originally a Brightlander has this experience. Because of this, I am asking of you a special request. Understand that this is a request and not a command. The King looked Raneous in the eyes. "It is this: that you go back to the Shadowlands and live there and continue to help my people. You could stay here and be a great war horse in the Heavenly Host, visiting the Shadowlands in times of battle but always returning to the Brightlands, or you can live in the Shadowlands and continue to learn how to hear My voice and fight the good fight everyday." The High King paused and let Raneous digest this. "It's up to you."

Raneous stood without moving looking at his beloved High King and then at all the incredible, clean and vivid beauty that surrounded him. With the fresh taste of apple still in his mouth, he thought of Brian and his mother. He thought of the pain and struggle they faced everyday just living in the mortal world. Brian and his mother were free now, but still new in the King's service. He looked over his shoulder and saw his mother, Radiance, waiting patiently to greet her long lost son. Leave? He just got here! But he was no longer a colt. He was a strong young stallion with valuable battle experience and apparently something unique to bring to the King's plan. He looked back at the King and took a deep breath, "I will return as you desire." Then he looked wistfully at him, "But can I come back to visit?"

The King smiled his wonderful smile of love, "You will not be forgotten and the door to the Brightlands will not be closed to you. However, there is something you need to know about the two realms. Here, we are outside of time and space. A day here could be a thousand days there. Once you are here you won't know where time is in the Shadowlands. You may find that no time has passed when you return, or you may find that years have passed." When the High King saw the look of consternation on Raneous' face, he added reassuringly, "Don't worry, I am the Creator of time and when you serve me it will be in the right time!"

Suddenly, the High King clapped his hands together two times and six small, giggling children jumped out from behind the trees as if they had been waiting there all this time. They ran to Raneous and three of them began lacing his beautiful white mane and tail with scarlet red ribbon while the other three began making joyful music on tiny silvery flutes. Horses, angels and more children began to gather around Raneous and the King at the sound of the merry tunes.

"Come now! You don't have to rush off quite yet. Let us

celebrate your homecoming! As a winged horse of heaven, you have earned great honor. I hereby bestow on you the Ribbons of Scarlet, for you have learned how to bring the presence of God into dark places!"

The Brightlanders cheered as Raneous stood happily beside his King in his new finery. Golden baskets of apples and oats were set out for the horses while the others enjoyed mouth watering cakes, luscious fruits, cheeses, and the finest wine. The children organized games of tag and hide and seek with the horses and angels. Soon, shouts of fun and laughter, punctuated by the rich, ringing laugh of the High King himself, rose out over the mountain meadows of the Brightlands.

So Raneous found himself surrounded by all whom he had ever known and loved, and best of all, he was able to bask in the presence of the High King. He felt new strength pour into his spirit. Joy flooded his soul just being with Him! He rested contentedly in the knowledge that he would be doing what the King asked him to do. Yet in all that joy, he looked around and he realized that he was missing someone. Brian! He suddenly missed Brian with a terrible ache. Tag was their favorite game together! Now he knew where his mission lay. He wanted more than anything for Brian to be able to celebrate with him - Brian and all the others that serve the High King. Raneous felt the passion and determination arise in his heart. "I will do whatever it takes to bring the lost home to the King for the biggest homecoming ever seen in all of history!"

The End of Book One

Index of Characters and Places

Characters:

Brian: an eleven year old boy who befriends Raneous. His father died a year ago and he is now dealing with his alcoholic uncle as his new step-father. He lives on a small farm in the Borderlands.

Brian's Mother: A kind, hard working woman who unexpectedly lost her husband in a farming accident. Unable to manage the farm on her own, she marries her husband's brother, Meldron.

Demons: A demon is a servant of the Evil One. The Bible says they are fallen angels and that they rebelled against God. In this story they are black and scaly with large talon-like claws and either yellow or red eyes.

Michael the Archangel: Michael is a real angel mentioned in the Bible. Michael leads God's armies against the Great Dragon's (Satan's) armies. He is a warrior and protector.

Palladon: (Pal-u-don) The swiftest and most powerful of the heavenly horses. He is a solid white, muscular war horse. He is ridden by Michael the Archangel, a champion horse of the Heavenly Host of Heaven, and the father of our hero, Raneous.

Radiance: A strong and beautiful gray mare with silver wings. She is a great warrior horse for the Heavenly Host of Heaven, and she is the wise and gentle mother of our hero, Raneous.

Raneous: (Ray-nee-us) A beautiful white winged colt, the son of Palladon and Radiance. In him is the strength of his father and the wisdom of his mother.

Rune: A mysterious red horse that has been disillusioned by his service to the High King.

The Evil One or The Great Dragon: Also known in this book as The Dragon. These are the names used in this book to represent Satan, the devil, the real biblical enemy of God.

The Heavenly War Host: The armies of heaven. They are the angels and winged horses that serve and fight for the protection of heaven and for the King's children.

The High King: The Creator of all worlds; the Captain of the Heavenly Host. The name used in this book to represent Jesus who became human and died so that we could be rejoined to our Father God.

Uncle Meldron: Brian's uncle who is now his stepfather. He is addicted to alcohol and has let it rule his life.

Vengol: A demon who serves under Captain Valtar in the Darklands. He is a servant of The Evil One, the Great Dragon.

Captain Valtar: A demon who serves the Evil One. He is the head demon in the region of the Darklands in which the story takes place.

Places:

Heaven: A real place in the spirit realm. This is where God and angels live. There is no evil in heaven. When a person is in heaven they can see God.

The Brightlands: The land of the winged horses, angels and others where all is pure and unspoiled by evil. It is in the heavenly realm but outside of heaven.

The Borderlands: This land is the part of the Shadowlands that is closest to the Darklands. It is the darkest place to be in the Shadowlands because the evil forces are strong there.

The City of Glory: The beautiful golden city where the High King and all his people live in heaven.

The Darklands: The land completely controlled by evil. In this book the Darklands go underground but it is also represented by massive dark clouds of complete blackness.

The Shadowlands: The land of mankind. It lies between the Brightlands and the Darklands. It has both good and evil in it and it is where the war for the King's children is being fought. It used to be unspoiled by evil, but now it is in constant war between evil and good.

ABOUT THE AUTHOR

Robin S. McDonald graduated from Bellarmine University, Kentucky with a degree in Secondary Education and English. She now lives with her husband, two daughters, an energetic dog and an ancient cat in the great state of Texas.

Robin has always enjoyed a good story - especially one that opens up the imagination to new ways of looking at life. Christian fantasy has been an important aspect of her growth as a person and as a Christian both as a child and as an adult. Ironically, fantasy has been the avenue that God used to demonstrate to her His amazing reality. Through fantasy, God revealed to her His creativity in this world.

"Winged Horse of Heaven" is her first published work and is to be Book One of the series "The Raneous Chronicles". This book is for both the young and the young at heart; the horse lover, the warrior, and all true servants of the High King.

Contact the author on Facebook at Robin S. McDonald-author, or at Raneouschronicles@gmail.com. This book is also available as an ebook.